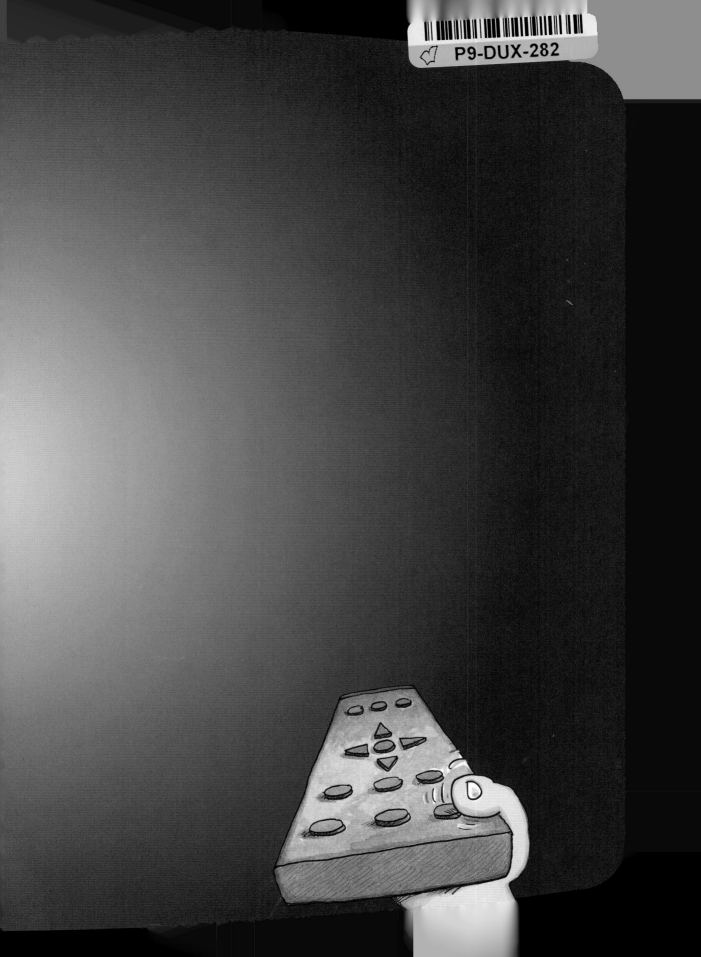

Date Due

PENNY LEE AND HER TV

Glenn McCoy

HYPERION BOOKS
FOR CHILDREN

New York

FIRST EDITION

1 3 5 7 9 10 8 6 4 2

Library of Congress Cataloging-in-Publication Data

McCoy, Glenn.

Penny Lee and her TV / Glenn McCoy.—1st ed.

p.   cm.

Summary: Penny Lee loves to watch television so much that she has no time for anything else, but one day when the television stops working, her dog Mr. Barkley shows her some of the other fun things they can do.

ISBN 0-7868-0661-3. (trade)

[1. Television—Fiction. 2. Dogs—Fiction.] I. Title: Penny Lee and her television. II. Title.

PZ7.M47841446 Pe 2002

[E]—dc21

00-54011

Visit www.hyperionchildrensbooks.com

Penny Lee loved her TV. She watched it all day long.

She had many favorite shows—about 300 of them.

She liked exciting outer-space shows like *Captain Laser Blazer from Planet X* and cute animal shows like *Pinky Poodle's Pool Party*. In fact, Penny Lee liked every show on TV.

In her right hand, Penny Lee held the TV remote. That was the hand with her clicking thumb. No one could click faster than Penny Lee.

Penny Lee didn't have any friends. She didn't need any. The TV was her best friend. It kept her company during rainstorms. It kept her warm on winter nights.

Penny Lee never left her TV. She ate her meals in front of it.

When she had to leave the room, the TV went with her.

The TV was on all day and night. Penny Lee even slept on top of it. And while she snoozed, her dreams would have commercial breaks.

Penny Lee had a dog named Mr. Barkley.
But she was too busy for him. Mr. Barkley tried
everything to get Penny Lee to notice him.
But it was no use.

One morning when Penny Lee awoke, she knew
something was wrong.

The TV screen was cold and dark.

"Help, Mr. Barkley!" Penny Lee cried. "I'm missing my morning shows!"

She tried the remote. She shook the TV, but nothing happened. "Help!" Penny Lee yelled. "Call 911! Call the fire department! Call the National Guard!!"

Mr. Barkley thought for a second and decided that this was his big chance.

Mr. Barkley turned all the knobs
on the TV and pressed all the buttons.
He walked around to the back
and jiggled the wires.

"Well?" Penny Lee said. "Is it serious? You've got to help me!"

Mr. Barkley picked up a newspaper and pointed inside. "A TV repair place!" she said. "I'll bet they can fix it!"

In a flash the three of them were out the door.

Penny Lee looked around as they walked. Everything was so bright and colorful. She was used to seeing everything on a screen. Penny Lee tried adjusting the color with her TV remote, but it didn't work.

Across the street Penny Lee saw some girls playing jump rope. Mr. Barkley took the TV cord and began twirling it. Penny Lee jumped rope between her two friends.

Suddenly, Penny Lee looked at her watch. "Oh, no, *Puppy Puppets Playhouse* comes on soon! We have to get to the repair shop!"

The three of them came to the
top of a steep hill. As they started
down, the TV began to roll.

At first Penny Lee was a little scared. Then she got over it.

She was missing her show, but she knew there was a better one on in a couple of hours.

When they got to the bottom, they played hide-and-seek.
Mr. Barkley had no trouble at all finding Penny Lee. After that
they built a kite.

Penny Lee looked at her watch again. She was missing the *Admiral Bubble Bath Show.* But she couldn't go home yet.

In the afternoon they went swimming in a pond.

Mr. Barkley taught Penny Lee how to do the dog paddle.

They went for a ride around the block.

They went fishing in a creek.

They drew pictures on the sidewalk.

They went to the library and read books to each other.

Finally, they lay in the grass and found
shapes in the clouds.

Penny Lee was exhausted.

Then Penny Lee realized that it was getting late.

"We've got to get to the repair shop!" she said.

When they got there, the store was closed.

Mr. Barkley waited for Penny Lee to get mad.

But instead she said, "Oh, well, I guess we'll come back tomorrow."

That night, when Penny Lee fell asleep,
her dreams were commercial free.

Mr. Barkley couldn't sleep at all.

He was too excited. He "fixed" the TV

and turned on a late-night movie.

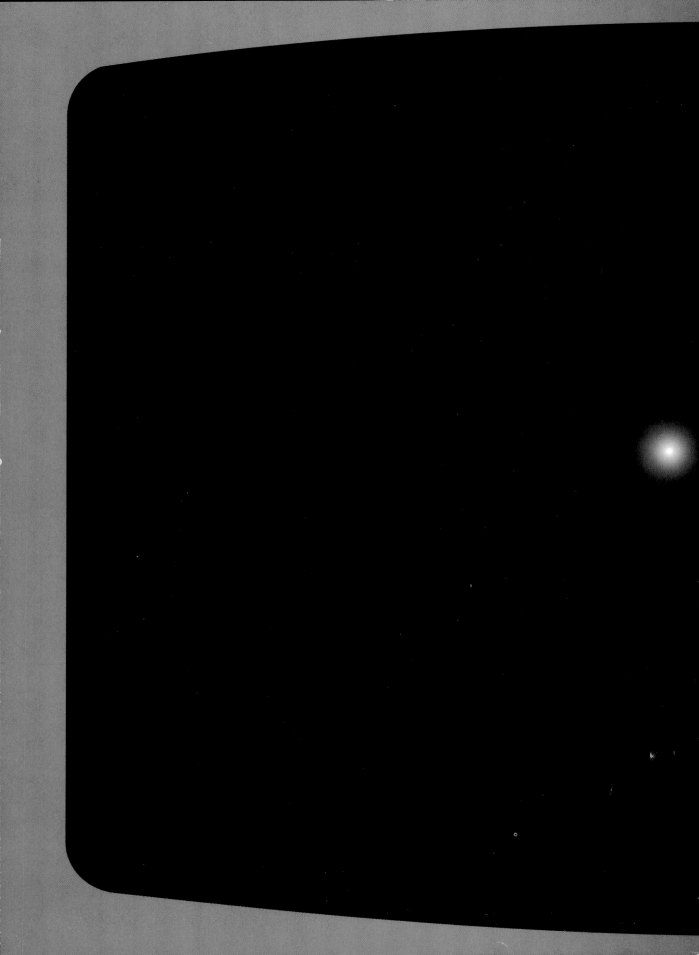